ANGEL IN DISGUISE

Laura Shenton

ANGEL IN DISGUISE

Laura Shenton

Iridescent Toad Publishing

Iridescent Toad Publishing.

This book is entirely a work of fiction. The names, characters and incidents portrayed in it are the work of the author's imagination. Any resemblance to actual persons, living or dead, events or localities is entirely coincidental.

Designations used by companies to distinguish their products are often claimed as trademarks. All brand names and product names used in this book and on its cover are trade names, service marks, trademarks and registered trademarks of their respective owners. The publishers and the book are not associated with any product or vendor mentioned in this book. None of the companies referenced within the book have endorsed the book.

Cover by Covers and Berries.

First edition. ISBN 978-1-913779-49-8

Chapter One

Calista Wright adjusted her worn canvas backpack as she emerged from the towering English Literature building at Westlake University. The late afternoon sun cast long, golden shadows across the sprawling campus, its amber light catching the edges of the weathered brick buildings that surrounded the central quad. She tucked a wayward strand of vibrant pink hair behind her ear with slender fingers – a nervous habit she'd developed over the years of trying to blend in. Her dyed hair – her small, carefully chosen act of rebellion against the conformity she otherwise embraced – contrasted sharply with her overall understated appearance: a faded grey t-shirt that had seen too many laundry cycles, worn jeans with a fraying hem, and scuffed canvas shoes that had carried her through countless lecture halls.

She looked like any other twenty-year-old university student navigating the daily academic grind, which was, of course, exactly the point.

What her classmates and professors didn't know – what nobody in her carefully constructed world could ever discover – was that beneath her meticulously maintained normalcy, Calista harboured a profound secret that weighed on her consciousness during every waking moment. Hidden from human perception – existing in a dimension just adjacent to the physical realm – were her wings. Magnificent, powerful, white-feathered appendages that extended nearly twelve feet when fully spread, their pristine surface occasionally revealing shimmers of iridescence when caught in certain light. Wings that undeniably marked her as something other than ordinary.

An angel walking among normals, hiding in plain sight.

She had dedicated most of her young life to keeping this extraordinary truth concealed, even from those who had come closest to breaching her carefully constructed emotional walls. The wings themselves weren't physically present in this dimension most of the time – they existed in what she referred to as the 'adjacent space', a parallel plane of existence that intersected with the everyday world – but she could manifest them into physical reality when absolutely necessary.

"Hey, daydreamer! Earth to Calista! Are you even on this planet right now?"

Calista snapped out of her recursive thoughts to see her flatmate and closest friend, Erica Butler, waving energetically at her from a wooden bench near the campus coffee shop, the aroma of freshly ground beans wafting through the air between them. At twenty-four, Erica was noticeably older than most of their undergraduate peers, having worked for several years before returning to university to finish her mathematics degree. Her keen, analytical eyes missed nothing about the people and world around her, which made her an excellent friend when Calista needed support – but also someone Calista had to be perpetually careful around, lest she reveal something she could never take back.

"Sorry," Calista said with a self-deprecating smile, crossing the manicured lawn to join her friend on the bench. "I was completely lost in thought about that Virginia Woolf essay due next week. The stream of consciousness technique is really messing with my analytical approach."

"Ultimate nerd," Erica replied with affectionate exasperation, gathering her thick mathematics textbooks and spiral notebooks. "Some of us are solving differential equations while others are pondering the symbolic meaning of waves breaking on the shore, or whatever." She checked her phone briefly before continuing, "I've got a gig tonight at The Underground. You're coming, right? I need at least one friendly face in the audience."

Erica's burgeoning side career as a stand-up comedian was steadily gaining momentum, her razor-sharp wit and take-no-prisoners observational style earning her a growing and devoted following in the city's competitive comedy scene. Her performances had become a bright spot in Calista's otherwise cautious existence.

"Wouldn't miss it for anything," Calista

promised, meaning every word. "You're finally using that new material about your probability professor with the bizarre chalk habits, aren't you?"

"Oh yeah. That man is a statistical anomaly of awkwardness and unconscious tics. Absolute comedy gold." Erica stood, brushing off her jeans and slinging her heavy bag over her shoulder with relaxed confidence. "I've got to run to the library before heading home – need to return these reference books before they charge me the GDP of a small nation. See you at the apartment around six? We can grab dinner before the show."

Calista nodded, watching her friend hurry off across the quad, her confident stride carrying her swiftly through groups of lingering students. She envied Erica's straightforward existence sometimes – the beautiful simplicity of it all. Normal problems, normal relationships, normal aspirations – they all seemed so... contained. Comprehensible. Manageable. Calista's own existence was perpetually complicated.

She knew only fragmented details about her heritage. Her mother had been entirely human, that much was certain. Her father –

well, he had quite literally been an angel, though Calista had never met him and knew almost nothing about his specific lineage or purpose. Her mother had shared cryptic stories and half-memories before she passed away when Calista was sixteen, but much of it sounded like romantic fantasy rather than practical, useful information about navigating life as a half-celestial being.

What Calista did know with certainty was that she wasn't fully either species. She possessed abilities beyond human capacity – enhanced strength that allowed her to lift objects three times her body weight, remarkable speed when necessary, heightened senses that could detect sounds and smells imperceptible to those around her, and occasional, frustratingly unpredictable visions – but she lacked the complete power, knowledge, and divine purpose of true angels. She existed in a liminal space, caught between worlds, belonging fully to neither realm.

She headed towards the campus bus stop, mentally planning to get home and change into something more suitable before heading to Erica's comedy show. The early evening air was pleasantly crisp, carrying the first subtle hints of approaching autumn as she walked along the tree-lined cobblestone path that meandered from the older, ivy-covered part of campus towards the main road where buses arrived every fifteen minutes.

That's when it hit her without warning.

A blinding white flash erupted behind her eyes, followed immediately by a disorientating cascade of vivid images – a small child with neatly done pigtails and a bright yellow backpack, a busy downtown intersection teeming with after-work pedestrians, a delivery truck with catastrophically failed brakes barrelling towards the crosswalk, terrified screams piercing the urban cacophony. Then precise geographic co-ordinates somehow imprinted themselves in her mind like a brand, identifying a location across the sprawling city, along with a specific time: exactly seventeen minutes from this moment.

Calista gasped, clutching her throbbing head as the vision gradually released its grip on her consciousness. She had experienced these unexpected premonitions before, but rarely with such intensity and clarity. They came without discernible warning or pattern, but one thing remained distressingly consistent: they always showed someone in imminent danger. Someone whose life hung in precarious balance. Someone she could help, if she chose to act.

She hated it with every fibre of her being.

These inconvenient visions inevitably forced her to use her supernatural abilities, to risk exposure in a world that would never understand what she was. But she couldn't simply ignore them either, couldn't pretend she hadn't seen what fate had revealed to her. Not when an innocent life – this time a young girl's – hung in the balance of her decision.

Calista checked her watch anxiously, performed a quick mental calculation of how long it would take to reach the precise location in her vision by conventional means, and cursed under her breath at the impossible mathematics of the situation. There was absolutely no time for buses, taxis, or any other human transportation.

She'd have to fly, revealing her true nature to the open sky, if not to human eyes below.

Looking around carefully to ensure she was completely alone, Calista quickly ducked behind the protective cover of a massive, ancient oak tree, its sprawling branches providing temporary sanctuary. She closed her eyes and focused her entire consciousness on the adjacent space, on the part of herself that existed beyond normal human perception. The familiar yet always strange sensation of her wings emerging from their extradimensional hiding place washed over her body – a peculiar feeling like stretching powerful muscles that had been painfully cramped for far too long. The substantial weight settled across her shoulder blades, simultaneously burdensome and paradoxically empowering, as the pristine white feathers materialised fully into the physical world, responding to her urgent need.

With a powerful, decisive thrust of her newly manifested wings, she launched herself skyward, staying strategically close to the protective tree line until she had safely cleared the university campus, then soaring higher into the darkening evening sky. The sprawling city spread beneath her like a living, breathing map of light and shadow as she accelerated towards the precise co-ordinates that remained seared into her mind with supernatural clarity.

She only hoped she would make it in time to prevent tragedy – and that no curious eyes would glimpse her impossible form against the twilight sky, revealing the secret she had guarded for her entire existence.

Chapter Two

Calista landed gracefully in a narrow alley two blocks from the intersection she'd seen in her vision, willing her wings back into the adjacent space – that mysterious dimension that housed parts of herself when they weren't needed in this world. The sensation rippled across her shoulder blades like a thousand pins and needles, uncomfortable but necessary, like forcing a limb to sleep. She rolled her shoulders, adjusting to the phantom weight that always lingered after her wings retreated. The brick walls of the alley rose around her, graffiti-tagged and weathered, as she checked her watch: three minutes to spare before catastrophe would strike.

She sprinted towards the busy intersection, her heart hammering against her ribs with such force she could feel each pulse in her throat. Her shoes slapped against the concrete, dodging pedestrians who barely registered her urgency. The scene materialised exactly as in her vision: the same chain coffee shop on the corner, the vintage clothing boutique with its mannequins posed in the window, the same harried pedestrians waiting impatiently at the crosswalk, checking phones and watches. And there – a little girl with chestnut pigtails, swinging her mother's hand back and forth, completely oblivious to the danger hurtling towards her.

Calista scanned the traffic with heightened senses, her vision sharper than any normal person's could be. She spotted the delivery truck that had featured prominently in her vision rounding the corner, its white paint gleaming. Even from this distance, her acute hearing picked up the driver's panic – the rapid increase in heartbeat, the stream of desperate prayers, the frantic pumping of brakes that weren't responding. Metal groaned in protest as the truck continued its unstoppable trajectory.

Time seemed to slow, stretching like treacle as Calista calculated the deadly course with mathematical precision. The truck would hit the crosswalk in approximately twelve seconds, exactly as the pedestrians began to cross. The little girl would be directly in its path, her tiny body no match for tons of metal and momentum.

People were already stepping off the curb as the pedestrian signal changed from red to white, a steady stream of humanity flowing into the street. The mother and daughter were nestled in the middle of the group, the woman distracted by her phone, the child skipping cheerfully beside her.

No time for subtlety or second-guessing.

Calista broke into a run, pushing her speed to its inhuman limit, muscles burning with supernatural energy. To bystanders, she would appear as little more than a blur, a rush of displaced air, perhaps a flicker in their peripheral vision. She reached the crosswalk just as the truck barrelled towards it, horn blaring in warning – a desperate, too-late attempt by the driver to alert pedestrians to the danger.

The little girl had stepped away from her mother, a few paces ahead, tugging at the stretched limit of their joined hands before breaking free entirely. She hopped onto a painted white line of the crosswalk, playing an improvised game of hopscotch, directly in the truck's path. The mother looked up from her phone, her expression morphing from distraction to dawning horror as she registered the oncoming truck and her daughter's position.

Calista had a split-second decision to make, calculations racing through her mind faster than any computer. She could attempt a rescue without revealing her nature, but the angles were wrong – the physics impossible. There wouldn't be enough time or leverage. The girl would be hit, her small body crushed beneath unforgiving wheels.

With a silent apology to her future self and everything she'd worked so hard to protect, Calista let her wings materialise in a surge of energy that tingled across her back. The familiar weight unfurled as she launched herself forward, the delicate yet powerful appendages catching the air with practiced precision. She scooped the child into her arms – so light, so fragile – and propelled them both into the air just as the truck skidded through the spot where the girl had stood, leaving black tire marks on the asphalt and the scent of burning rubber hanging in the air.

They hung suspended for a moment, ten feet above the intersection, caught in a pocket of stillness while chaos erupted below. Horns blared, people screamed, the truck finally ground to a halt after clipping a streetlight. The girl's eyes were wide with shock rather than fear, pools of innocent wonder in a round face. Her small hands instinctively grasped at Calista's shirt, fingers curling into the soft grey fabric.

"You're an angel," she whispered, her voice tinged with awe, her breath warm against Calista's collarbone.

Calista didn't respond, couldn't trust herself to find the right words in this moment of exposure. Instead, she focused on landing safely away from the unfolding chaos. Her wings beat once, twice, carrying them in a gentle arc to the opposite side of the street. She set the child down with deliberate gentleness next to her stunned mother on the sidewalk, painfully aware of the dozens of eyes fixed on her like spotlights – and the numerous phones raised to record the scene, their lenses capturing evidence she could never erase.

"Are you ok?" she asked the little girl, crouching to meet her eyes, searching for signs of trauma or injury. The child nodded, seemingly more excited than frightened, a smile playing at the corners of her mouth as if she'd just experienced the most thrilling playground ride.

"You saved her," the mother said, tears streaming down her face, carving glistening paths through her makeup as she clutched her daughter with trembling hands. "Thank you. Thank you." Her voice cracked with emotion, gratitude and disbelief mingling in equal measure.

A crowd was gathering now, a circle of shocked faces and pointing fingers, exclamations rising around them like a tide. "Did you see that?" "Those wings!" "Oh my God!" "It's a miracle!" Calista's pulse thundered in her ears, drowning out some of the voices but not enough of them. This was exactly what she had spent her entire life avoiding, the exposure she had been warned against since childhood. She needed to disappear, now, before questions could be asked that she couldn't answer.

"I'm glad she's safe," Calista said, already backing away, gravel crunching beneath her shoes. "Please, take care." Her voice sounded strained even to her own ears, tight with the effort of appearing calm when every instinct screamed at her to flee.

Before anyone could approach her, before the paralysis of shock could wear off and allow someone to reach for her, she turned and ran, wings still visible and partially extended behind her. She knew she couldn't hide them again until she was out of sight – the process required concentration she couldn't spare while running. She heard shouts behind her, people calling for her to wait, to come back, curiosity and wonder giving their voices an edge of desperation.

She ducked into an alley between a laundry and a convenience store, the narrow passage offering momentary shelter from prying eyes. With a powerful downbeat of her wings that sent debris swirling in miniature cyclones, she leapt upward and took flight, staying low between buildings until she was far enough away to risk climbing higher. She hugged the shadows of fire escapes and water towers, banking sharply around corners, using every trick she'd practiced in secret to minimise her visibility.

Only when she was soaring above the city, high enough that she would appear as nothing more than a large bird to casual observers below, did she allow herself to process what had just happened. The wind rushed past her face, whipping her hair back and cooling the flush of exertion and fear that had heated her skin.

She was exposed. Maybe not personally – no one had seen her face clearly enough to identify her, she hoped – but her existence, the existence of something not entirely human, was now indisputable. There would be video evidence spreading across social media already, being shared and re-shared, analysed and debated, with each viewing increasing the risk of someone recognising her.

Calista flew home by a circuitous route, cutting across neighbourhoods and doubling back occasionally to ensure she wasn't being followed – a paranoid habit that suddenly seemed entirely justified. Eventually, she landed on the flat tarred roof of her apartment building, a converted warehouse in a rapidly gentrifying neighbourhood where artists and students lived alongside young professionals and trendy start-up employees. She made her wings vanish in a shiver of energy before climbing down the rusting fire escape to the window of the apartment she shared with Erica, the metal creaking softly beneath her weight.

Thankfully, the apartment was empty. Calista needed that time alone to think, to plan, to figure out how to contain the damage she had caused.

She turned on the TV with shaking hands, flipping to the local news channel. As expected, she was already the lead story, her worst fears confirmed in high definition.

"Breaking news: An apparent angel rescues child from certain death," the reporter announced, his professional demeanour cracking slightly with disbelief, an emotion she could see him struggling to suppress. "Amateur footage shows a young woman with wings saving a six-year-old girl from being struck by an out-of-control delivery truck at the intersection of Fifth and Maple."

The screen filled with shaky phone footage of Calista's rescue, her wings clearly visible as she lifted the child to safety, the feathers catching the city's light in a way that made them almost glow. Her face was mostly obscured by her hair and the angle of the shot, but it was still the most exposed she had ever been. The footage looped, playing again and again as the reporter continued speaking, each repetition hammering home the reality of her situation.

The reporter continued, his voice steady but his eyes wide with wonder: "The unidentified woman disappeared before authorities arrived. Police and emergency services are asking for any information about this mysterious guardian angel. The child, Emma Phillips, was unharmed and is home with her family, who have expressed their profound gratitude and desire to thank the woman personally."

Calista sank onto the couch, her legs suddenly unable to support her weight, her hands shaking uncontrollably. The reporter continued, interviewing witnesses who described the "miracle" they had seen, experts weighing in on whether the footage could be authentic or was some elaborate hoax, religious leaders offering their interpretations of what an angel's appearance might mean for humanity.

"The city is buzzing with speculation," the reporter concluded, shuffling his papers in a gesture that seemed almost quaint given the extraordinary nature of the story. "Who is this angel among us? And why has she chosen to reveal herself now?"

Calista turned off the TV, her thoughts racing like frightened birds trapped in a small room. She had saved a life – that was what mattered. But now she faced a new danger: discovery. If she were identified, her life as she knew it would be over. Best case scenario, she'd become a curiosity, hounded by media and researchers, never again knowing a moment's peace. Worst case? She'd become a specimen, detained in the name of science or religion, her autonomy stripped away along with her freedom.

She couldn't let that happen. Somehow, she had to contain this situation before it spiralled completely beyond her control, before her identity was uncovered, before others like her might be put at risk by her carelessness.

The sound of keys jangling in the door made her jump, her nerves raw and oversensitive. Erica was home, her familiar footsteps crossing the threshold.

"Cal? You here?" Erica called, dropping her bags by the door with a heavy thud. "Have you seen the news? It's absolutely wild. Some kind of angel or something saved a kid downtown. Everyone's losing their minds about it." Her voice grew louder as she entered the living room, then faltered as she caught sight of Calista. "What's wrong? You look like you've seen a ghost."

Calista forced a smile that felt brittle on her face, hoping it looked more natural than it felt. "Just tired. And yeah, I saw the news. It's... pretty unbelievable." She tried to keep her voice casual, but could hear the strain in it, the slight tremor that betrayed her agitation.

Erica flopped onto the couch beside her, the cushions shifting beneath her weight. The scent of coffee and library books clung to her clothes. "The footage looks genuine. I mean, as a sceptic, I want to say it's fake, but the multiple angles, the consistency... it's compelling." She glanced at Calista, her eyes curious. "What do you think?"

"I don't know what to think," Calista said carefully, weighing each word. "It's definitely strange." She focused on keeping her breathing even, on not fidgeting, on all the little tells that might betray her.

"Strange is an understatement," Erica replied, pulling out her phone, the blue light illuminating her face. "It's trending everywhere. 'Angel in Disguise', they're calling her, because she was dressed so normally. Jeans and a grey shirt." She squinted at her phone, scrolling through what must have been endless commentary. "Actually, kind of like what you're wearing. Weird coincidence."

Calista's heart stuttered, missing a beat before resuming at a faster pace. "Yeah. Weird." She resisted the urge to change her clothes immediately, knowing it would only draw attention.

Erica was still scrolling through her phone, oblivious to Calista's inner turmoil. "They're offering a reward now for information. The girl's parents want to personally thank her rescuer. There's going to be a press conference tomorrow."

"A press conference?" Calista echoed, unable to keep the alarm from her voice. A press conference meant more attention, more eyes searching, more chances for someone to recognise her.

"Yeah. The mayor's involved now. It's become this whole city thing." Erica glanced up, her expression thoughtful. She turned her attention back to her phone, thumb swiping rapidly through content. "Oh my God, they've got clearer footage now. Someone had a better angle." She held up her screen, the video playing on a loop. "Can you see the wings? They look so real."

Calista glanced at the video, then quickly away, her stomach clenching. It was a clearer shot than what had been on TV, though her face was still mostly hidden by her hair and the downward angle of her head. "Very convincing," she managed to say, fighting to keep her voice steady.

"I need to use this in my set tonight," Erica said, standing and stretching, seemingly energised by the day's events. "This is perfect material. Angel in the city? Come on." She headed towards her bedroom, her enthusiasm palpable. "I should get ready. You still coming to the show?"

"I... I'm not feeling great, actually," Calista said, seizing the opportunity for solitude. "I might stay in tonight." The thought of sitting in a crowded comedy club, hearing Erica joke about the very thing that might destroy her life, was unbearable.

Erica paused at her bedroom door, concern crossing her features. "You sure? You do look a bit pale. Everything ok?"

"Just a headache. Maybe a bug or something." Another lie, small but necessary.

"Alright, rest up then." Erica disappeared into her room, calling back, "I'll tell you all about it tomorrow!"

Alone again, Calista buried her face in her hands, pressing her fingers against her closed eyes until colourful patterns swirled in the darkness. This was exactly what she had feared her entire life, what her mother had warned her about. Now it was happening, and she had no idea how to contain it, how to put this particular genie back in its bottle.

One thing was certain: she needed to be more careful than ever. No more rescues, no matter how compelling the vision. No more risks. No one could connect Calista Wright, ordinary literature student with the battered paperback of Tennyson in her bag, with the 'Angel in Disguise' who had saved Emma Phillips.

Her very freedom depended on it.

Chapter Three

By morning, the story had exploded beyond Calista's worst fears. She woke to find Erica already in the kitchen, the TV in the living room tuned to the local news where a press conference was in progress. The mayor stood at a podium, his expression solemn yet excited, flanked by Emma Phillips and her parents, along with stern-faced police officials and what appeared to be religious leaders from various faiths – their diverse ceremonial attire creating a tableau of shared purpose that made Calista's stomach clench.

"The city of Westlake is offering a substantial reward for information leading to the identification of the individual who saved young Emma's life," the mayor was saying, his voice carrying the practiced gravitas of a politician seizing a moment in the spotlight.

"We wish only to express our gratitude and to understand the extraordinary circumstances of yesterday's events. This is a moment of profound significance for our community."

Emma's father stepped to the microphone next, his face haggard yet hopeful, his eyes rimmed with the remnants of tears and sleeplessness. "To the angel who saved our daughter: we just want to thank you. You've given us the greatest gift imaginable – our child's life. Please, come forward on your own terms. We respect your privacy and your... unique situation." His voice caught on the last words, a blend of awe and uncertainty that reflected the city's collective bewilderment.

Calista sank into a chair at the breakfast bar, her stomach knotting with dread as Erica handed her a steaming cup of coffee, the aromatic bitterness doing little to settle her nerves. The cup trembled slightly in her grasp, tiny ripples forming on the dark surface of the liquid.

"Wild, isn't it?" Erica said, gesturing at the TV with a slice of toast in hand, crumbs scattering across the counter. "My show was packed last night. Standing room only at the comedy club. Everyone was talking about it. The angel is officially Westlake's hottest topic."

"How did it go?" Calista asked, desperate to shift the conversation away from the angel, from herself, from the secret that now felt like it was burning a hole through her chest with each passing moment.

"Nailed it," Erica replied with a self-satisfied grin, dropping onto the stool beside Calista. "My angel material got the biggest laughs of the night. I did this whole bit about how if I had wings, I'd use them for way more selfish purposes, like never dealing with traffic again, or sneaking into concerts, or spying on my exes from cloud height." She wiggled her eyebrows suggestively.

Calista forced a laugh, the sound hollow even to her own ears. "Sounds funny. Wish I could have been there." She wrapped her hands tighter around the warm cup, seeking comfort in its solidity while her world seemed increasingly unmoored.

"You feeling better today? You were pretty out of it yesterday." Erica's eyes narrowed slightly, scanning Calista's face with the perceptiveness that made her both a good friend and, at this moment, a potential threat to Calista's secret.

"A bit," Calista lied, attempting to inject some vitality into her voice. In truth, she'd barely slept, her mind racing with scenarios of discovery and exposure, each more catastrophic than the last. The few moments of rest she'd managed had been plagued by dreams of being hunted, of wings failing mid-flight, of falling endlessly while cameras flashed around her.

"Good, because we've got plans." Erica tapped rapidly on her phone, then held it up to show Calista a social media post, the screen a blur of exclamation points and hashtags. "They're organising a city-wide 'Thank You Angel' event this afternoon. Flash mob style. People are gathering at all the major intersections downtown at three o'clock, wearing white and holding thank you signs. The post already has thousands of shares. Thought we could go – front row seats to mass hysteria."

Calista nearly choked on her coffee, the liquid burning a path down her throat as she struggled to maintain composure. "Why would we do that?" she asked, setting the cup down with excessive care to hide the tremor in her fingers.

Erica raised an eyebrow, her expression a mixture of amusement and mild concern. "Because it's literally the biggest thing to happen in this city... ever? Because it'll be hilarious to see all these people losing their minds over a possible supernatural entity? Because I need new material for my next set?" She ticked off the reasons on her fingers. "Take your pick."

"I've got that paper due on Monday," Calista hedged, grasping for excuses. "Victorian literature and its treatment of the supernatural. I should really work on that. I've barely started the research." The irony of the topic wasn't lost on her – analysing fictional otherworldly beings while hiding her own supernatural nature.

"It's Saturday! Come on, live a little. The paper can wait." Erica started pulling up more information on her phone, her enthusiasm undeterred. "They're setting up the main event at the intersection where it happened.

They've got permits for a temporary stage, sound system, the works. The news says they're hoping the angel will make an appearance if enough people gather. They're calling it a 'beacon of community gratitude' to draw her out."

Calista felt a chill run down her spine, goosebumps rising on her arms beneath her long-sleeved pyjama top. "That seems... unlikely," she murmured, imagining the spectacle with a growing sense of dread. The thought of hundreds of people gathered specifically to summon her made her feel simultaneously hunted and revered – neither sensation comfortable.

"Obviously. But it'll still be entertaining." Erica glanced up from her phone, her expression softening slightly. "Unless you really are still feeling sick? You're looking a bit pale again."

The concern in her friend's voice made Calista feel guilty about her deception. Erica had always been there for her, through late-night study sessions and personal crises alike. Now Calista was shutting her out, hiding behind half-truths and vague excuses. "No, it's not that. I just... don't see the appeal, I guess. Seems like a lot of commotion over what was probably just someone in a costume, or a trick of the light. Mass hysteria, like you said." She struggled to keep her tone casual, dismissive.

"The appeal is in witnessing mass cultural hysteria in person," Erica said with a laugh that echoed too loudly in their small kitchen. "Think of it as anthropological research for that social contexts in literature course you're always going on about. How often do you get to see a modern myth being born? Besides, the footage is pretty convincing – that was either the best cosplay ever or something truly weird."

Calista recognised that Erica wouldn't easily let this go. And refusing too adamantly might raise suspicion, might cause her friend to wonder why she was so determined to avoid the event. "Fine," she conceded with a sigh that she hoped sounded put-upon rather than terrified. "But just for a little while. And I need to get some work done before we go."

"Perfect!" Erica clapped her hands together, the sharp sound making Calista flinch. "Wear something white. I'm going to make a sign. I'm thinking 'Angels Are Real, Deal With It' in glitter letters. Too much?"

"Never too much glitter for an angel sighting," Calista replied with forced lightness, her attempt at humour falling flat to her own ears.

As Erica bustled around the apartment, gathering craft supplies with the enthusiasm of a child preparing for a school project, Calista retreated to her bedroom, closing the door softly behind her. Panic rose in her throat, constricting her breathing as she leaned against the door, eyes closed. She was being drawn into the very spectacle created around her secret identity, like a moth circling ever closer to a flame. What if someone recognised her? What if she ran into Emma or her parents? What if they looked into her eyes and somehow saw the truth?

She sat on the edge of her bed, hands pressed to her chest, trying to steady her breathing. This was temporary, she told herself. The furore would die down eventually. People would move on to the next sensational story. She just needed to lie low, play along, and wait for it all to blow over. It wasn't as if the footage was clear enough for anyone to make a positive identification. At least, that's what she desperately hoped.

An important email alert pulled her from her thoughts, the cheerful chime incongruous with her sombre mood. She picked up her phone, expecting a message from Erica with more event details, but instead saw Dr Mercer's name. Her Victorian Literature professor had written: *Calista, could you come by my office this afternoon? There's something important I'd like to discuss.*

Calista stared at the message, her anxiety spiking further, blood rushing in her ears. It was unusual to get a text from a professor on a weekend, especially one as formal and traditional as Dr Mercer. Had Dr Mercer somehow recognised her in the footage? The thought seemed paranoid, but Calista couldn't dismiss it entirely. The professor was notoriously observant, with an almost uncanny ability to notice details most people missed.

I have plans this afternoon, she replied after a moment's hesitation, fingers hovering over each letter before committing. *Could we meet Monday before class?*

The response came quickly – almost too quickly – as if Dr Mercer had been watching her inbox, waiting: *This is rather urgent. I wouldn't ask otherwise. It concerns a matter of mutual interest.*

Mutual interest. The phrasing seemed deliberate, loaded with potential meaning. After another moment's hesitation, Calista wrote back: *I can come by around 1pm. Is everything ok?*

Perfect. See you then. And yes, everything is fine. Just a matter requiring discretion. The last word sent another wave of unease through Calista's body.

Calista set down her phone, her mind racing through possibilities, most of them alarming. It could be about her coursework, certainly. Perhaps an issue with her last paper. But the timing felt too coincidental to ignore. Dr Mercer's office was in the old humanities building on the edge of campus – not many people would be around on a Saturday. If the professor had somehow identified her, this meeting could be a trap.

But it could also be a chance to gauge how much danger she was in. Knowledge was power, after all. Better to know what Dr Mercer suspected than to wonder and worry. And if the professor did know something, perhaps Calista could convince her to keep the secret. Dr Mercer was known for her eccentricity, her fascination with the Victorian obsession with the supernatural and paranormal. Maybe she would be more intrigued than alarmed by Calista's nature.

"Hey, what time is your meeting with that professor?" Erica called from the living room, her voice cutting through the door and shattering Calista's thoughts. "We should co-ordinate so we can head downtown together afterwards."

Calista stepped out of her bedroom, confused. "How do you know about that meeting?"

Erica gave her an odd look, pausing in her crafting to study Calista's face. "You just said it out loud while you were messaging. You were muttering about having to go to campus. Are you sure you're ok? You seem really distracted. If you're still sick, we can skip the whole thing."

"Sorry," Calista said, forcing a smile that felt plastic on her face. "Just stressed about that paper. And yeah, maybe still a bit under the weather. The meeting shouldn't take long though. I can meet you downtown once I've finished. No need to wait for me."

"Perfect! I'll send you the location. I'm meeting some friends there early to get a good spot near the stage." Erica returned to her sign-making, humming contentedly, glitter already dusting her hands.

Calista retreated back to her room, trying to recall if she'd actually spoken aloud while messaging. She didn't think so, but she was scattered enough that maybe she had. She needed to be more careful. Her secret was already in enough danger without careless slips.

She spent the next hour attempting to work on her paper, but the words on her laptop screen blurred and shifted, refusing to coalesce into coherent thoughts. Her mind kept returning to the impending meeting with Dr Mercer, to the crowds gathering downtown, to the search for the mysterious angel – for her. Eventually, she gave up on productivity and began preparing for her meeting, selecting clothes with careful deliberation – casual enough for a weekend, but neat enough to project seriousness and stability. The last thing she needed was to appear nervous or erratic.

At a quarter to one, Calista left for campus, promising to meet Erica at the downtown event afterwards. The walk to Dr Mercer's office gave her time to compose herself and prepare for various scenarios. She tried to think of plausible explanations in case the professor confronted her with suspicions. Deny involvement. Claim a case of mistaken identity. Perhaps suggest a lookalike relative or doppelgänger. None of the excuses seemed particularly convincing, even to her own mind.

Chapter Four

The humanities building was quiet, its labyrinthine hallways empty, most offices dark and locked for the weekend. The quiet intensified every small sound – Calista's footsteps on the worn marble floors, the hum of the ancient heating system, the distant slam of a door. Dr Mercer's light was on, the door ajar, a sliver of warm yellow light spilling into the dimly lit corridor. Calista knocked softly, her knuckles barely grazing the weathered wood.

"Come in, Calista," Dr Mercer called, her voice calm and measured.

The professor was seated behind her desk, glasses perched on her nose as she reviewed some papers. In her fifties, with silver-streaked dark hair pulled into a neat bun and sharp, intelligent eyes, Dr Mercer had a reputation for brilliance and eccentricity in equal measure. Her office reflected this duality – meticulously organised bookshelves alongside curious artefacts and mysterious trinkets collected from her travels. The space smelt of old books, tea, and a hint of something herbal and unfamiliar.

"Thank you for coming on such short notice," she said, gesturing to the comfortable chair opposite her desk. "Please, sit. Would you care for tea? I've just brewed a pot."

"No, thank you," Calista replied, not trusting her unsteady hands with a delicate teacup. She sat, hands folded tightly in her lap, knuckles white with tension. "Is everything alright with my coursework? My last paper..."

"Your academic performance is exemplary, as always," Dr Mercer replied, removing her glasses and setting them aside with deliberate care. "That's not why I asked you here." She leaned forward slightly, her elbows resting on the antique desk, fingers steepled before her. "I wanted to talk to you about yesterday's incident downtown."

Calista's heart stuttered, missing a beat before resuming at a faster tempo. "Oh?" The single syllable emerged higher than intended, a nervous squeak that she tried to disguise with a small cough.

"Yes. The angel sighting." Dr Mercer's gaze was uncomfortably direct, her eyes seeming to peer beyond Calista's carefully constructed façade. "I found it fascinating on multiple levels, not least because it echoes so many of the themes we've been discussing in our Victorian literature course. The intersection of the divine and the mundane, the struggle between concealment and revelation. The Victorians were obsessed with angels, you know – messengers between realms, creatures of profound ambiguity."

"It is an interesting parallel," Calista said carefully, her mind racing to interpret Dr Mercer's angle. Was this academic curiosity, or something more targeted? "I hadn't considered the connection to our readings."

Dr Mercer nodded, a slight smile playing at the corners of her mouth. "Indeed. But more personally, I found it fascinating because the angel in question bears a striking resemblance to one of my most promising students." Her voice remained conversational, but there was a weight to her words that settled in the room like a physical presence.

The office seemed to grow colder, the air thickening around Calista. She maintained her neutral expression with effort, years of hiding her true nature coming to her aid in this crucial moment. "I'm not sure I understand," she said, the words feeling clumsy and inadequate even as she spoke them.

"I think you do, Calista." Dr Mercer's voice was gentle, almost kind, creating a dissonance with the potentially devastating content of her words. "I've been watching the footage rather obsessively since yesterday. The physical similarities are remarkable – the height, the build, the distinctive way the hair falls. But more telling is the way she moves – fluid yet hesitant, as if constantly holding back. It's the same way you carry yourself in class, like someone perpetually afraid of taking up too much space."

Calista's mind raced through her options, weighing each potential response. Denial seemed safest, the instinctive retreat of the cornered, but something in Dr Mercer's tone gave her pause. There was no hostility there, no eagerness for exposure or sensationalism. No recorder visible, no phone positioned to capture her reaction. Just genuine curiosity and what seemed like concern.

"Even if that were true," Calista said slowly, each word chosen with deliberate care, "why would you tell me this? Why not go to the authorities or the media? The reward must be substantial." The question was a test, a probe to reveal the professor's motivations.

"Because I understand the desire for privacy," Dr Mercer replied without hesitation, as if she had anticipated the question. "And because I believe I can help you navigate this situation. You're in a precarious position, whether you acknowledge it or not."

"Help me how?" Calista couldn't keep the scepticism from her voice.

Dr Mercer stood, moving with graceful purpose to a bookshelf where she retrieved an old, leather-bound volume, its spine cracked with age, its corners worn smooth by generations of handling. "I have some knowledge of individuals who exist… outside the ordinary spectrum of humanity." She returned to her desk and opened the book, revealing handwritten notes and exquisitely detailed drawings. "My grandmother kept detailed records of her encounters throughout her life. She was what some might call a scholar of the extraordinary, at a time when such interests were dismissed as feminine hysteria or superstition."

Calista stared at the pages, which contained meticulously rendered sketches of beings with wings – not the cartoon angels of popular imagination, but anatomically complex structures that looked unsettlingly similar to her own. Alongside them were careful observations written in faded ink, diagrams, pressed flowers, and what appeared to be feather samples preserved between tissue-thin pages. "Why are you showing me this?"

"Because you need allies, Calista. The city is in a frenzy. Everyone is looking for the angel – some with good intentions, others with motives far less pure." Dr Mercer closed the book with reverent care. "If you are who I think you are, you saved a child's life at great personal risk. That speaks to your character. I have no interest in exposing you to the world's scrutiny, but I do want to offer my assistance in navigating what comes next. This won't simply disappear, no matter how much you might wish it to."

Calista hesitated, considering her options, balancing the risk of trust against the potential benefit of having someone knowledgeable in her corner. Dr Mercer seemed sincere, and having an ally – especially one with knowledge of beings like her – could be invaluable. But trust had never come easily to her, not since she'd first discovered her difference, her otherness, in her formative years.

"What exactly are you offering?" she asked finally, neither confirming nor denying the professor's suspicions, maintaining the thin veneer of hypothetical discussion.

"Information, for starters. My grandmother's records contain accounts of others like you – or at least similar to you. Historical sightings, personal testimonies, theories about origin and purpose. You might find answers to questions you've been afraid to ask. And practical support. A safe place to retreat if necessary. Help managing your public identity. Guidance on controlling your... visibility." The last word carried clear meaning beyond the literal.

Calista studied her professor's face, searching for any sign of deception or ulterior motive. The office was quiet, the only sounds the ticking of an antique clock and the distant hum of campus machinery. "Why would you do this?" The question emerged softer than intended, vulnerability seeping through.

"Intellectual curiosity, in part," Dr Mercer admitted with a candid shrug. "I've spent my academic career studying the Victorian fascination with the supernatural, never truly expecting to encounter it myself. But also because I believe extraordinary individuals should be protected, not exploited. My grandmother taught me that. She harboured several unusual guests during her lifetime, keeping their secrets even from her own family. I discovered her writings on it only after her death."

After a long moment of consideration, Calista made her decision. Complete denial seemed pointless now, but full confession felt equally dangerous. She would test the waters cautiously. "If – hypothetically – I were this angel, what would you suggest I do about the current situation?"

Dr Mercer smiled slightly, the expression warming her features. "Hypothetically? I'd suggest controlling the narrative. Right now, others are defining who and what this angel is – a divine messenger, an alien, a superhero, a hoax. Speculation runs rampant in the absence of facts. Perhaps it's time she spoke for herself, on her own terms. Defined her own identity before others solidify their interpretations."

"That sounds dangerous," Calista said, unable to keep the alarm from her voice. The thought of deliberately stepping into the spotlight made her physically recoil. "Exposure could lead to... consequences." Unwanted attention. Scientific scrutiny. Religious fanaticism. The possibilities were endless and uniformly terrifying.

"Less dangerous than being discovered unprepared," Dr Mercer countered, her tone gentle but firm. "Right now, you're reacting, not acting. Always on the defensive. It's exhausting and ultimately unsustainable." She leaned forward slightly. "But we don't have to decide anything immediately. This situation will continue to evolve. Think about it, consider your options. Observe how the public narrative develops." She held out the leather-bound book. "And take this. It might provide some perspective, some context for your... unique situation."

Calista accepted the book with hesitant hands, feeling its weight, its history. She tucked it carefully into her bag, aware of its value both as an artefact and potentially as a key to understanding herself better. "Thank you. I'll consider what you've said."

"That's all I ask." Dr Mercer checked her watch, a delicate vintage piece on a slender chain. "I believe there's an event downtown soon. If our hypothetical angel wanted to observe how the city is responding to her appearance, that would be the place to do it. Knowledge is power, Calista, especially when navigating uncharted territory."

Calista nodded, standing to leave, suddenly eager to escape the professor's gaze and the intensity of their conversation. "I did promise my friend I'd meet her there. She's quite excited about the whole thing."

"Be careful, Calista," Dr Mercer said softly, the words following her to the door. "And remember, you're not alone. Not anymore."

Chapter Five

As Calista left the humanities building, stepping from its cool, musty interior into the crisp autumn air, her mind was spinning with this unexpected development. Dr Mercer's recognition of her was concerning, evidence that she wasn't as anonymous as she'd hoped, but her offer of alliance was strangely comforting. For the first time since the incident, since she'd spread her wings in public view, Calista felt a glimmer of hope. Maybe she didn't have to face this entirely on her own, didn't have to carry the burden of her secret in solitude.

She texted Erica, confirming she was on her way downtown, trying to infuse her message with an enthusiasm she didn't feel. As she walked towards the bus stop, she kept her head down, hoodie pulled forward to shield her face, hyperaware of the people around her, wondering if anyone else might recognise her from the blurry footage that had captivated the city's attention.

The city had changed overnight, transformed by a collective obsession with the angelic apparition. Angel imagery was suddenly everywhere – hastily printed t-shirts in shop windows, posters taped to lampposts, street art spray-painted on alley walls. Calista's face – or rather, the angel's face – stared back at her from every direction, rendered in various artistic interpretations that, thankfully, bore only passing resemblance to her actual appearance. The abstraction of these images was a small mercy; artists had seized the limited visual evidence and filled in the gaps with their imagination, creating versions that ranged from the ethereally beautiful to the unnervingly alien.

She was heading towards a celebration of herself, walking among people searching for her. The irony wasn't lost on her as she boarded the crowded bus, squeezing between passengers wearing shirts emblazoned with wing designs and slogans like 'I Believe' and 'Angels Among Us'. She hunched smaller in her seat, the leather-bound book a comforting weight against her side, a promise of answers to questions she'd been afraid to even formulate.

As the bus approached downtown, the crowds grew denser, the atmosphere charged with a peculiar energy – part religious revival, part carnival, part protest. Calista could see people gathering at intersections, many wearing white as requested, some with wings fashioned from cardboard or fabric strapped to their backs. Signs reading 'Thank You, Angel' and 'We Believe' dotted the sea of people. Street vendors had appeared, opportunistically selling angel merchandise – pins, pendants, hastily produced pamphlets about angelic encounters throughout history.

Calista texted Erica again, fingers trembling slightly on the screen: *Where exactly are you? It's packed down here. Can barely move through the crowd.*

Main intersection where it happened, came the reply, accompanied by a dropped pin on a map. *Near the makeshift stage. Look for my 'Angels Are Real, Deal With It' sign. It's purple with silver glitter. You can't miss it unless you're literally blind.*

Calista made her way through the crowd, tension coiling in her stomach, a serpent of anxiety tightening with each step. Being here was reckless, she knew, but somehow necessary. She needed to understand what she was facing, needed to see first-hand the impact of her momentary decision to reveal her true nature. The book in her bag seemed to grow heavier, a physical manifestation of the weight of her secret.

She spotted Erica's purple sign bobbing above the crowd, a beacon of garish glitter against the sea of white attire, and worked her way towards it, murmuring apologies as she squeezed between tightly packed bodies. Her friend was in animated conversation with a stranger, gesturing emphatically, her performer's voice carrying over the ambient noise.

"Calista!" Erica called when she spotted her, waving enthusiastically. "You made it! How was the meeting?"

"Fine," Calista said, glancing around nervously, cataloguing exit routes and potential hiding spots out of habit. "Just about my paper topic. She had some suggestions for sources." The lie came easily enough.

"Well, you're just in time. They're about to start the official thank-you ceremony. Emma and her parents are here. The mayor too. Even some scientists from the university – probably hoping to explain away the miracle." Erica rolled her eyes at this last part.

Indeed, on the hastily constructed stage, Emma Phillips stood with her parents, the family at the centre of the unfolding drama looking simultaneously overwhelmed and determined. The little girl clutched a drawing she had made, the paper fluttering slightly in the autumn breeze. She wore a white dress, her hair tied back with a ribbon that matched, looking like a miniature angel herself in the afternoon sunlight. The mayor approached the microphone, raising his hands for quiet, his political instincts clearly recognising the career-defining potential of this moment.

"Citizens of Westlake," he began, his amplified voice echoing across the hushed crowd, "we gather today to celebrate a miracle in our midst and to express our collective gratitude to the mysterious guardian who saved young Emma's life yesterday." He paused, allowing the weight of his words to settle over the assembly. "In a world often darkened by tragedy and division, this moment of grace reminds us of the possibility of the divine touching our everyday lives."

The crowd cheered, the sound overwhelming in its intensity, a wall of noise that made Calista want to cover her ears, to flee from the sensory assault. She felt dizzy with the strangeness of it all, with the surreal experience of hearing herself discussed as a supernatural entity while standing anonymous in the very crowd searching for her.

"We may not understand the nature of the being who came to Emma's aid," the mayor continued once the cheering subsided, his rhetoric polished and practiced. "But we recognise the pure goodness of that act. And so we gather, as a community, to say thank you – and to extend an invitation. Wherever you are, whatever you are, you have friends in this city. You have nothing to fear from us.

We wish only to express our gratitude and perhaps, if possible, to understand."

Another cheer went up, louder than before, a sound of collective affirmation that rippled through the crowd like a wave. Emma stepped forward to the microphone, her mother helping her adjust it to her height, the child's expression solemn with the importance of the moment.

"Thank you for saving me, angel lady," she said simply, her small voice made huge by the amplification system. "I was really scared when that truck was coming, but then you were there, and I wasn't scared anymore. I made you a picture." She held up her drawing of a figure with pink hair and white wings, rendered with the earnest imprecision of childhood art. "I hope you can come and get it. And I hope you're not too scared that people know about you now."

Calista felt tears pricking at her eyes, a lump forming in her throat, moved despite her fears. The sincerity in the child's voice cut through her anxiety, reminding her of why she had acted in that crucial moment – not for recognition or acclaim, but because a life was in danger and she had the power to save it. Would she make the same choice again, knowing the consequences? She wasn't sure, and that uncertainty troubled her more than the exposure itself.

"They're going to release white balloons now," Erica said, nudging Calista with an elbow, pulling her from her thoughts. "Environmentally questionable, but visually effective. Internet gold, for sure."

Sure enough, hundreds of white balloons were being distributed through the crowd, passed from hand to hand with reverent care. "Write your message to the angel," people were instructed as volunteers moved through the assembly with markers. "Tell her what you want her to know."

Erica scribbled something on her balloon, then handed the pen to Calista. "Here. Your turn. Make it good – who knows, maybe she'll actually read it." She laughed at the impossibility, unaware of the irony of her words.

Calista stared at the balloon in her hand, marker hovering over its taut surface. What message would she write to herself? What words could capture the complexity of her situation?

Finally, she wrote simply: *You are not alone.* The words were as much for herself as for her angelic persona.

"That's oddly profound, Cal," Erica said, peering over her shoulder with casual curiosity. "You getting emotional about all this?"

"It's just... moving," Calista replied, surprised by how true it was, how deeply she was affected by this outpouring of gratitude and wonder. "All these people coming together for something positive, something hopeful. It's rare." She blinked rapidly, willing away the moisture in her eyes before it could betray the depth of her emotion.

"On three, we release the balloons!" the mayor announced, his voice carrying across the crowd. "One... two... three!"

Hundreds of white balloons rose into the blue sky, carrying messages of appreciation and awe, a floating monument to the city's collective amazement. Calista watched them ascend, a visual metaphor for the situation spiralling beyond her control, rising and dispersing on currents she couldn't navigate. The crowd applauded as the balloons became distant white specks against the vast canvas of sky, like inverse stars appearing in daylight.

Emma's father took the microphone, his expression more determined than his daughter's had been. "We're not giving up," he said firmly, a hint of steel beneath the gratitude in his voice. "We'll keep searching until we find our angel. If you're watching this, please know that we only want to thank you properly. You can trust us. We will respect whatever boundaries you set."

Calista felt a cold certainty settle over her as she listened to his words, as she surveyed the sea of eager faces surrounding her. This wasn't going to blow over, wasn't going to fade from public consciousness in a few days as she had hoped. The search wouldn't stop. The interest wouldn't wane. Eventually, someone would connect the dots – if Dr Mercer had figured it out so quickly, others could too.

She needed to make a decision about how to handle this situation. Dr Mercer's advice about controlling the narrative echoed in her mind. Perhaps a strategic, limited revelation on her own terms would be safer than being exposed by others with their own agendas.

"You ok, Cal?" Erica asked, noticing her expression. "You look weird."

"I'm fine," Calista said automatically. "Just overwhelmed by the crowd."

Erica nodded, then suddenly grabbed Calista's arm. "Oh my God. Look who's here."

Calista followed Erica's gaze to where a group of university students had gathered, among them Jackson Reed, the campus newspaper editor who fancied himself an investigative journalist.

"He's got his camera," Erica observed. "Probably doing a story on all this."

Calista watched as Jackson photographed the crowd, the stage, and the celebratory merchandise. His ambition was well known; breaking the identity of the angel would be exactly the kind of story he'd pursue relentlessly.

"I think I need some air," Calista said, suddenly feeling claustrophobic. "It's too packed here."

"It's an outdoor event, Cal. This is air." But Erica's sarcasm faded when she saw Calista's face. "Hey, seriously, are you ok?"

"I just need a minute. I'll text you." Before Erica could protest further, Calista pushed her way through the crowd, away from the main intersection, away from the cameras and the searching eyes.

She found a quiet alley and leaned against the wall, breathing deeply. Dr Mercer's words echoed in her mind: *Perhaps it's time she spoke for herself.*

Could she do that? Reveal herself on her own terms? The thought was terrifying but also strangely liberating. Living in perpetual fear of discovery was its own kind of prison.

But before she could consider it further, she heard a familiar voice nearby.

"I'm telling you, I've seen her before." It was Jackson Reed, speaking to someone just around the corner. "Something about her is familiar."

"Everyone's seeing the angel everywhere now," another voice replied dismissively. "Mass hysteria."

"No, this is different. I've been going through campus photos from the newspaper archives, and I swear I've seen that profile, that hair colour before."

Calista froze. Jackson was methodically searching for her, and he had resources and determination on his side. It was only a matter of time before he found something concrete.

Heart pounding, she slipped away before they could round the corner. The situation was accelerating faster than she had anticipated. She needed to make a decision, and quickly.

She texted Erica: *Not feeling well. Going home. Sorry.*

Then she found a secluded spot and did the one thing she had promised herself she wouldn't do again: she let her wings materialise and took to the sky, staying high enough to avoid easy detection, circling the city as she tried to sort through her options.

Below her, the 'Thank You Angel' event continued, citizens searching for a miracle while the miracle herself soared unseen above them, trying to find the courage to face so many unknowns.

Chapter Six

Calista spent hours flying above the city, watching as the crowds eventually dispersed from the thank-you event. From this height, people looked like miniature figures in a diorama, their concerns and excitements reduced to tiny movements, their voices mere whispers lost in the wind. The buildings, once imposing, became simple geometric shapes – concrete and glass arranged in neat patterns below her. It was easier to think up here, where the air was clear and cold, where the constant noise of humanity faded to a distant hum, where she could be herself without fear of discovery or judgment.

The sky had shifted through shades of blue as the afternoon progressed, now deepening towards early evening. Wispy clouds drifted past her, occasionally enveloping her in their cool embrace. Each time she passed through one, moisture collected on her skin and feathers, a gentle reminder of her place between worlds – not fully of the earth below, yet still bound to it.

Dr Mercer's book was in her bag, pressed against her as she soared. The weight of it, physical and metaphorical, stayed with her through each graceful turn and dive. She was eager to read it, to see if it contained answers to questions she'd had her entire life – questions that had lingered in her mind since childhood, multiplying as she grew older and became more aware of her difference. But first, she needed to decide her immediate course of action, to formulate a plan that wouldn't leave her exposed and vulnerable.

Jackson Reed was actively investigating, his journalistic instincts having led him uncomfortably close to the truth. Dr Mercer had already figured out her identity with surprising ease. It seemed inevitable that others would too, given enough time and determination. Each person who connected the dots brought her closer to a full revelation. The question was whether to wait passively for that to happen, allowing others to control the narrative, or to take control of the situation herself, dictating the terms of her emergence into public knowledge.

As twilight descended over the city, painting the horizon in strokes of orange and purple, Calista finally returned to the ground, landing in a deserted park several miles from her apartment. The grass was still warm from the day's sun, contrasting with the growing coolness of the air. A few joggers passed in the distance, oblivious to her presence in the deepening shadows beneath a cluster of oak trees.

In her normal human form, she found a secluded bench, partially hidden by overgrown shrubbery, and sat down, her muscles pleasantly tired from the extended flight. She opened Dr Mercer's book carefully, mindful of its fragility. The leather was cracked with age, the binding loose in places, the pages yellowed and brittle, their edges worn soft from decades of handling. They carried the faint scent of old paper and something else – perhaps lavender or another herb. She turned them carefully, scanning the handwritten entries. The penmanship was elegant but practical, the ink faded from black to sepia in places, especially on pages that appeared to have been exposed to sunlight.

The journal spanned decades of encounters with what Dr Mercer's grandmother called 'liminal beings' – creatures that existed at the threshold between mundane reality and something else, entities that straddled the border between the scientifically explicable and the mysterious. There were detailed accounts of meetings with individuals possessing extraordinary abilities: a man who could manipulate fire with a precision that defied physics, a woman who communicated with the dead through touch, claiming to feel residual energies, and, yes, several entries about winged beings who could manifest and retract their feathered appendages at will.

One passage in particular caught Calista's attention, the handwriting becoming more hurried and excited, as if the writer had been unable to contain her enthusiasm:

17th April 1952 – Met again with E., the young man with wings. Our conversation lasted well into the night, the longest yet. He explained more about their nature – they exist simultaneously in our dimension and another, which he calls the 'adjacent space'. This allows them to manifest or conceal their wings at will, though the process seems to require concentration and deliberate intent. E. believes he is only half-angel, his mother having been human. He struggles with his dual nature, feeling he belongs fully to neither world, forever caught between identities. I sense great loneliness in him despite his remarkable gifts. When he speaks of flight, his eyes light up with a joy that quickly dims when he mentions the necessity of hiding.

Calista's breath caught, her heart pounding. The description matched her experience so precisely that it was unsettling – like discovering a diary entry about herself, written by a stranger decades before she was born. Her fingers trembled ever so slightly as she continued reading:

E. says there are others like him, though they are rare and typically live in isolation to avoid detection. Some find remote areas – mountains, deserts, quiet coastlines – where they can unleash their wings more frequently without fear of discovery. He fears what would happen should his nature become widely known – persecution from religious zealots who would view him as blasphemous, experimentation by scientists eager to understand biological impossibilities, exploitation by those who would use his abilities for their own ends, whether political, military, or commercial. Yet he also speaks of a deep yearning for connection, for understanding, for the simple pleasure of being known truly and accepted completely. He helps people when he can, using his abilities secretly. It seems to bring him some measure of peace, a way to give purpose to gifts that otherwise isolate him.

A jogger passed near her bench, causing Calista to instinctively hunch over the book, shielding it from view. She waited until the footsteps faded before relaxing again. The park was growing darker, the paths now lit only by intermittent lamps that cast pools of yellow light at regular intervals.

She flipped through more pages, finding scattered references to E. and others like him throughout the journal. According to these accounts, half-angels often had unique abilities beyond their wings – enhanced strength that manifested in moments of need, periodic visions that offered glimpses of people in danger, accelerated healing that puzzled physicians – but these powers manifested inconsistently and were sometimes difficult to control, especially during periods of emotional distress or physical exhaustion.

One final entry about E. made Calista's heart ache with recognition of a pain she had carried her entire life:

3rd October 1954 – E. has decided to leave the city. The strain of concealment has become too great, he says. He fears his wings will manifest involuntarily during moments of stress or emotion, exposing him to scrutiny and danger. There have been close calls – a sudden manifestation during a thunderstorm that frightened him, an almost-discovery by a neighbour who entered his apartment unannounced. When I asked where he would go, he spoke vaguely of "somewhere less crowded, less observant", his eyes distant as if already seeing forests or mountains far from prying eyes. I tried to persuade him that he could find acceptance, that there were people who would understand, but his fear runs too deep, born of a lifetime of careful hiding. I wonder if all those with extraordinary gifts are doomed to such isolation, or if there might come a time when our world is ready to embrace rather than fear the exceptional among us. I will miss our conversations, the privilege of witnessing something miraculous in my otherwise ordinary life.

Calista closed the book slowly, her mind swirling with implications. The journal felt heavy in her hands, burdened with both revelation and confirmation. E. had grappled with the same dilemmas she now faced, the same fears that haunted her – and he had chosen to retreat, to isolate himself, to disappear. But that was the 1950s, when differences of any kind were less tolerated, when the world was still recovering from war and suspicion ran deep. Could things be different now, in an age of greater acceptance and understanding? Or would the hunger for sensation, for exploitation, for control be even greater?

The vibration of her phone interrupted her thoughts, its screen illuminating her immediate line of sight in the growing darkness. Multiple texts from Erica, each progressively more urgent:

Hey, you ok?
You've been gone for hours. I'm getting worried.
Please text back so I know you're alive.
Seriously, Cal, where are you?
At least let me know you haven't been kidnapped or something.

And then, sent just a minute ago:

You need to get home NOW. That campus reporter Jackson just showed up at our door asking questions about you. Said he thinks you might know something about the angel. I told him you were sick in bed but he didn't believe me. He's coming back with his editor. This is weird and I'm freaking out.

Calista's stomach dropped, a cold sensation spreading through her chest. Jackson was already at her doorstep, moving faster than she had anticipated. Events were accelerating beyond her control, the luxury of careful deliberation evaporating.

She texted back quickly, fingers flying across the screen: *I'm fine. On my way. Don't let anyone in. No matter what they say.*

Then she stood, tucking the precious journal securely into her bag. She looked around carefully to ensure she was alone; the entire area was now nearly deserted as evening settled fully over the city. Satisfied, she stepped into a deeper shadow beneath an ancient oak and took flight again, her wings emerging smoothly from the adjacent space, powerful and eager after their brief rest.

The city spread beneath her, a glittering tapestry of lights now that darkness had fallen. She flew swiftly, navigating by familiar landmarks, moving higher where necessary to avoid detection. The cool air rushed past her face, sharpening her focus. She needed to get home before Jackson returned with reinforcements, before the situation could escalate further.

Chapter Seven

Landing silently on the roof of her building, Calista retracted her wings, feeling them fold back into the adjacent space with a sensation like stretching a muscle in reverse. She glanced around to ensure no one had witnessed her arrival, then hurried down the fire escape, her footsteps deliberately light on the metal stairs. When she reached the window of her apartment, she tapped lightly on the glass, peering through to see Erica pacing the living room, phone in hand.

Erica's expression shifted from worry to relief as she recognised Calista's face in the darkness. She opened the window with quick movements. "Where the hell have you been? And why are you coming in through the window like some kind of cat burglar?"

"It's a long story," Calista said, climbing inside and ducking to avoid hitting her head on the window frame. "What exactly did Jackson say?"

Erica closed the window behind her, locking it securely before turning to face Calista, arms crossed over her chest, a mixture of concern and exasperation on her face. "He said he's been reviewing footage from the angel incident, comparing it with campus photos, social media, everything he could get his hands on. He thinks you either know her or..." She hesitated, her expression suggesting the next words were difficult to say. "Or you are her. Which is obviously ridiculous. I mean, I told him you don't even like heights."

Calista opened her mouth, then closed it again. No words came. She glanced away, tracing the intricate pattern of the carpet, as if the answer might be hidden there.

Erica's eyes widened, the annoyance fading, replaced by something like dawning comprehension. "It *is* ridiculous, right? Cal?"

Calista sank onto the couch, the weight of the moment pressing down on her like a physical force. Their apartment suddenly seemed smaller, the walls closer, as if the enormity of what she was considering couldn't be contained in such an ordinary space. "What would you say if it wasn't?"

"What do you mean?" Erica sat beside her, confusion evident on her face, the cushion dipping slightly between them.

"If it wasn't ridiculous. If I was..." Calista couldn't finish the sentence, the words sticking in her throat after years – her entire life – of careful silence.

Erica stared at her, comprehension dawning slowly, her eyes searching Calista's face for any sign of jest or deception. "Calista, are you trying to tell me that you're..." She shook her head, as if refusing to complete the thought. "No. That's not possible."

"Why isn't it possible?" Calista asked quietly, meeting her friend's gaze steadily despite the fear churning in her stomach.

"Because I've known you for nearly two years. Because..." Erica trailed off, continuing to study Calista's face with growing wonder and uncertainty. "Holy wow! You're serious."

Calista nodded slowly, feeling as if she were moving underwater, everything slow and dreamlike. "I've never told anyone. Not ever. Not once."

Erica stood up, pacing the living room, her sock-covered feet silent on the worn carpet. She ran her hands through her hair, a habit Calista knew indicated intense thought or stress. "This is insane. You're telling me my flatmate, who steals my cereal and forgets to pay the electric bill, who cried watching that documentary about penguins, is some kind of... supernatural being?"

"Half," Calista corrected automatically. "My mum was human. Completely human."

Erica stopped pacing, turning to stare at her, arms falling to her sides. "Can I see?"

The challenge hung in the air between them. Calista hesitated, then stood, pushing aside a floor lamp to create more space. "Step back a bit. Please."

Erica complied without question, her expression caught between shock and anticipation, moving until her back was against the wall. Calista closed her eyes, concentrated on the familiar sensation of reaching into the adjacent space, and let her wings emerge – slowly, carefully, mindful of the apartment's tight quarters and the fragile objects surrounding them.

The white feathers materialised gradually, like a photograph developing, extending several feet on either side of her body, their tips nearly touching the walls. They glowed softly in the lamplight, each feather distinct and perfect. Erica's sharp intake of breath was audible in the sudden silence that fell between them.

"Oh my God," she whispered. "They're real. You're real."

Calista opened her eyes, watching her friend's reaction anxiously, prepared for fear, disbelief, even revulsion. "Are you afraid?"

"Afraid?" Erica moved cautiously, hand outstretched, as though approaching a wild animal – with respect and wonder rather than fear. "Can I...?"

Calista nodded, and Erica gently touched one wing, fingers brushing against the feathers with delicate precision.

"They're warm," she said, wonder in her voice. "And so soft." Her fingers traced the edge of a primary feather, her touch gentle. She looked up at Calista's face, her own expression transformed by awe. "Why didn't you tell me?"

"I've never told anyone," Calista repeated, the enormity of this moment washing over her. "I was taught to hide, to be afraid of what would happen if people knew. My mother was... protective. Fearful. She'd seen how people treated difference."

Erica stepped back, her hands falling to her sides, processing. "So that was you? *You* saved that little girl?"

Calista nodded, her wings shifting slightly with the movement, catching the light differently. "I sometimes get visions – glimpses of people in danger. Not often, but when they come, they're intense, undeniable. I can't control when they come, but when they do, I can't ignore them. It's like... a pulling sensation, here." She touched her sternum. "Like someone calling my name from far away."

"And now everyone's looking for you." Erica sat down heavily on the arm of the couch, her expression cycling through amazement, concern, and something like excitement. "The whole city is talking about the angel. Including Jackson Reed, who's apparently sharper than I gave him credit for." She looked up suddenly as if remembering. "He's coming back, Cal. With his editor. What are you going to do?"

It was the question Calista had been asking herself, turning it over like a stone in her mind: what Dr Mercer had suggested in her careful, measured way, and what the journal entries about E. had illuminated – a choice between perpetual hiding and controlled revelation.

"I think..." She hesitated, the magnitude of the decision weighing on her, her wings unconsciously folding closer to her body. "I think I need to stop running. To face this on my own terms."

"What does that mean, exactly?" Erica leaned forward, elbows on her knees.

"It means I need to control the narrative, like Dr Mercer said." Seeing Erica's confused expression, Calista quickly explained her meeting with the professor earlier that day, the woman's recognition and surprising acceptance, her suggestion that secrecy might no longer be possible or even desirable.

"So she recognised you too," Erica said thoughtfully, tucking a strand of hair behind her ear. "Cal, if multiple people are figuring it out independently, it's only a matter of time before it becomes public knowledge anyway. At least if you take control of the situation, you can set the terms. Choose who knows what, and when."

Calista paced the room, her wings folding back carefully to avoid knocking over lamps, picture frames, and the potted plants that Erica insisted on keeping despite her lack of gardening skills. "But what if it goes wrong? What if they want to study me, or use me somehow? What if some religious group decides I'm a demon, or the government wants to experiment on me? What if..."

"What if people just want to thank you?" Erica interrupted, standing to intercept Calista's nervous pacing. "From what I've seen, most people just want to thank you. You saved a kid's life, Cal. That little girl is alive because of you." She placed her hands on Calista's shoulders, looking directly into her eyes. "And you won't be alone. You've got me. And your professor. People who care about *you*, not what you can do."

Calista felt tears threatening, blurring her vision. The prospect of acceptance – of no longer carrying her secret alone like a heavy stone in her chest – was overwhelming after years of careful concealment.

A knock at the door made them both jump, the sound sharp and authoritative in the quiet apartment.

"Erica? It's Jackson. I've got my editor with me. We really need to talk to you – and Calista, if she's back."

The two women exchanged glances, an entire conversation passing between them without words. Erica looked at Calista questioningly, leaving the decision entirely in her hands. "What do you want to do?"

Calista took a deep breath, then closed her eyes, concentrating on the sensation of folding her wings back into the adjacent space. The familiar feeling of compression washed over her, a momentary pressure followed by lightness. When she opened her eyes, she looked like an ordinary student again, no different from thousands of others across the city.

"Let's talk to them," she said, her voice steadier than she felt, a new determination forming within her. "But not about everything. Not yet. I need to think about how to do this right."

Erica nodded and went to open the door. Jackson stood there with an older man Calista recognised as his faculty advisor from the journalism department, Professor Callahan, whose reputation for integrity was well-known on campus. Both men looked intensely curious, their eyes scanning the apartment as soon as the door opened.

"Sorry to bother you again," Jackson said, trying to peer around Erica, his expression eager and slightly nervous. "But this is important."

"Calista's back," Erica said, stepping aside to let them in, her tone deliberately casual. "She's been resting. She wasn't feeling well earlier."

Jackson and his advisor entered the apartment, their eyes immediately finding Calista on the couch. Jackson seemed disappointed to see such an ordinary scene – just a tired-looking student in casual clothes, nothing angelic or extraordinary about her.

"Calista," Jackson began without preamble, his enthusiasm momentarily checked by the mundane reality before him, "I've been analysing footage from the incident with the angel. Your height, build, and hair colour are a perfect match."

Calista kept her expression neutral, aware of Erica's supportive presence beside her. "Is there a question in there somewhere, Jackson?"

"Do you know who the angel is?" Jackson asked directly, his notebook already open, pen poised. "Or are you somehow connected to what happened? Were you there?"

Calista chose her words carefully, aware that whatever she said now might be quoted later, might become part of a story she couldn't control. "I'm aware of the incident, obviously. The whole city is talking about it. But I don't see why you think I'd have any special knowledge."

Jackson pulled out his phone, showing her a split screen of the angel footage and a campus newspaper photo from months ago, Calista partially visible in the background of a group shot at a poetry reading. "The resemblance is striking. Same height, same build, same hair colour."

"Lots of people have pink hair," Erica interjected, her tone deliberately dismissive. "It's hardly unique. There are at least three other students on campus with similar styles."

"It's more than the hair," Jackson insisted, his enthusiasm returning. "It's the way she moves, the profile..." He looked directly at Calista, his expression intense. "What were you doing yesterday afternoon?"

"I was sick," Calista said, the lie coming easily after years of similar deceptions.

The advisor, who had been quiet until now, studying Calista with thoughtful eyes, finally spoke up. His voice was measured, authoritative but kind. "We're not trying to harass you, Calista. But if you do know something, this could be an important story. We would handle it respectfully."

Calista studied them both carefully. Jackson was eager, ambitious – he wanted the scoop, the story that would launch his career beyond the campus newspaper. But his advisor seemed more respectful, genuinely curious rather than exploitative. There was wisdom in his gaze, experience that tempered enthusiasm.

"If – hypothetically – someone knew something about the angel, why should they trust you with that information?" she asked, her tone even. "The media isn't exactly known for respecting privacy. For handling sensitive stories with care."

"Because we're not just media, we're journalists," the advisor replied, his tone earnest. "Ethical journalism isn't about exploitation; it's about truth. And sometimes, controlling how a truth emerges is as important as the truth itself. Setting boundaries, establishing parameters."

The words echoed Dr Mercer's advice from earlier that day, the synchronicity striking Calista forcefully. She glanced at Erica, who gave her a subtle nod of encouragement, invisible to their visitors.

"I need time to think," Calista said finally, making a decision. "If I did know something – hypothetically – I wouldn't be ready to discuss it right now. Not without considering all the implications."

Jackson looked disappointed, but his advisor nodded understandingly. "That's fair. Here's my card." He reached into his jacket pocket, producing a business card that he handed to Calista. "If you change your mind, contact me directly. My email and phone number are on there. We could discuss parameters, boundaries. Off the record, until you decide otherwise."

After they left, Erica locked the door behind them, engaging both the deadbolt and the chain for good measure. She turned to

Calista, leaning against the door. "So? What are you thinking?"

Calista examined the business card, turning it over in her fingers. The paper was thick, high quality, the embossed lettering elegant. "I'm thinking I need to talk to Emma and her parents first. Before any journalists. They were part of this before it became a news story. They deserve that much."

"How would you even arrange that without revealing yourself? It's not like you can just call them up and say, 'Hey, I'm the angel who saved your daughter, mind if we chat?'"

"Dr Mercer might be able to help." Calista pulled out her phone. "She has connections throughout the city."

Erica sat beside her on the couch, close enough that their shoulders touched. The casual contact was reassuring, a reminder that despite everything that had been revealed, some things remained unchanged. "Whatever you decide, I'm with you. Though I have to say, finding out my flatmate is half-angel is not how I expected this weekend to go."

Calista smiled for what felt like the first time all day, the expression easing some of the tension she'd been carrying. "If it helps, I still plan to pay my half of the electric bill."

"You'd better," Erica said with a laugh, nudging Calista's shoulder with her own. "Angel or not, I'm not subsidising your excessive use of the hair dryer. Though I do have some questions about the wings. Do they need special grooming? Is that why you take such long showers?"

The banter felt normal, grounding, a reminder that extraordinary revelations could co-exist with ordinary friendship. Despite the enormity of what had been revealed, their relationship remained unchanged – or perhaps even strengthened by this new honesty between them. It gave Calista hope that others might respond similarly, seeing her as a person first, a curiosity second.

She emailed Dr Mercer, her fingers moving quickly over the screen: *I need your help arranging something. Can we meet tomorrow?*

The reply came quickly, as if the professor had been waiting: *My office, 10am. I'll bring coffee. The good kind from that place on Elm, not the faculty lounge sludge.*

Calista set down her phone, a plan beginning to form in her mind. It wasn't fully developed yet, more fragments and instincts than a coherent strategy, but it had shape and direction. She wouldn't run like E. had in the 1950s, disappearing to some remote location to live in perpetual solitude. She wouldn't hide forever behind careful lies and evasions. But she would approach this revelation carefully, on her own terms, with allies at her side.

The world now knew angels existed. Soon, they would meet one face to face. Not as a fleeting vision in a moment of crisis, but as a person with thoughts, feelings, fears, and hopes of her own.

Chapter Eight

Sunday morning dawned clear and bright, the sky a perfect azure blue. The vast, limitless expanse stretched overhead like an inviting canvas, unmarred by clouds. Calista had slept surprisingly well, the oppressive weight of her long-kept secret partially lifted by Erica's unexpected yet wholehearted acceptance.

Dr Mercer was waiting patiently in her office as promised, two steaming coffee cups positioned carefully on her desk. "You look better today," she observed thoughtfully as Calista entered the warm, book-lined room. "More resolved. There's a certain determination in your eyes that wasn't there yesterday."

"I am," Calista confirmed, taking the offered chair and wrapping her slender fingers around the warm paper cup. "I've decided to reveal myself, but carefully, methodically, in well-considered stages. I want to start with Emma and her parents. They deserve to know first, privately, before anyone else. After what they've been through – what we've been through together – they deserve that much."

Dr Mercer nodded approvingly, her eyes reflecting years of careful observation. "I suspected you might come to that conclusion after reading my grandmother's journal. Did you find it helpful?"

"Very helpful," Calista replied, shifting slightly in her chair. "Especially the detailed entries about E. They made me realise I'm not the first to face these impossible choices. There's something profoundly comforting about that – knowing someone else has walked this path before." She took a contemplative sip of her coffee, the rich aroma filling her senses. "Do you know what happened to him? After he left the city? Did he find what he was looking for?"

"My grandmother lost track of him for many years," Dr Mercer said, her voice tinged with a hint of melancholy. "But they reconnected unexpectedly in the 1970s. He had been living in a remote area, isolating himself from society as he'd meticulously planned. But he found it... hollow. Desperately empty in a way he hadn't anticipated. Eventually, he settled in a small, close-knit community where he revealed himself to a few trusted individuals. Not everyone, certainly, but enough that he no longer had to live entirely in hiding, constantly vigilant against discovery." She smiled slightly, the corners of her eyes crinkling with the expression. "He found a balance, which I suspect is what you're seeking as well. A middle ground between total secrecy and complete exposure."

"Exactly," Calista agreed, feeling a surge of validation wash over her. "I don't want to become a public spectacle, a curiosity to be examined and dissected by strangers, but I can't keep living in this perpetual fear of discovery either. Especially now that people are actively looking for me and constructing theories. The narrative is already forming without my input."

"So, Emma and her parents first," Dr Mercer said thoughtfully, tapping her finger lightly against her coffee cup. "I might be able to help facilitate that. A trusted colleague of mine in the psychology department knows the family's pastor quite well. We could arrange a private meeting through him, somewhere secure and neutral where you'd feel comfortable."

Calista nodded gratefully, relieved to have such thoughtful support. "And after that crucial first step, I think I want to speak with Jackson and his academic advisor. Control the emerging story rather than have it control me, shape the narrative before others can."

"A wise, strategic approach," Dr Mercer commented, her tone appreciative. "When were you thinking of setting these wheels in motion?"

"Today, if at all possible," Calista said firmly, her voice steady despite the butterflies swirling in her stomach. "Before I lose my nerve or talk myself out of it."

Dr Mercer raised an eyebrow but didn't question Calista's urgency. "I'll make some calls immediately. Give me an hour to arrange things properly."

While Dr Mercer worked her professional connections, Calista returned to the apartment to find Erica hunched intently over her laptop, designing what appeared to be a professionally formatted website.

"What are you doing?" Calista asked curiously, peering over her friend's shoulder at the screen.

"Creating your comprehensive online presence," Erica replied without looking up, her fingers flying skilfully across the keyboard. "If you're going public with this extraordinary revelation, you absolutely need to control your digital footprint from the very beginning. This is just a template at this point – very basic, nothing published yet. But ready when you are, for whatever you decide to share with the world."

Calista stared at the screen, deeply touched by Erica's proactive support. The simple yet elegant design featured a tasteful header reading 'Angel in Disguise' and ample space for carefully curated text and meaningful images.

"You really are completely ok with all this,

aren't you?" Calista said softly, almost whispering the words.

Erica finally looked up, her expression serious and unflinchingly direct. "Of course I am, without reservation. You're still you, Cal. Still the same person who burns toast and forgets to buy milk and stays up too late reading Victorian novels. Just with... accessories." She grinned mischievously. "Really awesome, spectacular accessories that I'm insanely jealous of, but still fundamentally accessories to the person I already know and care about."

Calista's phone buzzed urgently with an email from Dr Mercer: *Meeting successfully arranged. 2pm at St Mark's Church. Small chapel in the back, very private. Pastor Williams will personally bring the Phillips family. They don't know precisely why yet, just that someone has important information about the angel.*

Calista showed the message to Erica, her heart beginning to race. "It's really happening. Today. In just a few hours, everything changes."

"What are you going to wear?" Erica asked, suddenly practical and fashion-conscious. "I mean, do you go full angel mode, or keep it casual and approachable, or something in between?"

It was such a normal, quintessentially Erica-like question that Calista laughed despite her mounting nerves. "I think just regular me. Everyday clothes. The wings themselves will make enough of a dramatic statement without theatrical costuming."

"Fair point," Erica conceded. She closed her laptop decisively. "Want me to come with you for moral support? You shouldn't have to face this monumental moment alone."

Calista hesitated momentarily, then nodded with genuine appreciation. "If you really don't mind. It would help tremendously to have a familiar face there."

"Wild horses couldn't possibly keep me away," Erica declared emphatically. "This is literally the coolest, most extraordinary thing that has ever happened to me by association. I'll be telling my grandchildren about this day."

Chapter Nine

The hours until the momentous meeting passed both agonisingly slowly and alarmingly quickly. Calista changed her outfit three times before finally settling on simple dark-wash jeans and a soft blue button-down shirt – presentable but not trying excessively hard. The more fundamentally human she appeared otherwise, she reasoned carefully, the less overwhelming her magnificent wings would seem by contrast.

Dr Mercer met them precisely on time at the church, which was peacefully quiet on Sunday afternoon after the morning services had concluded. Pastor Williams, a kind-faced man in his fifties with gentle eyes and greying temples, greeted them warmly at the side entrance.

"Dr Mercer explained that this is an exceptionally sensitive matter," he said, his voice low and reassuringly calm. "The Phillips family are waiting patiently in the chapel. They're understandably curious about why they've been asked to come on short notice."

"Thank you for arranging this unusual meeting," Calista said sincerely. "I know it's rather unconventional and mysterious."

The pastor smiled gently, his expression compassionate. "In my considerable experience, most truly important, life-changing things are distinctly unusual. I'll take you to them now without further delay."

He led them down a short, carpeted hallway to a small, intimate chapel, warm and inviting with magnificent stained glass windows casting kaleidoscopic coloured light across the polished wooden pews. Emma sat fidgeting between her attentive parents in the front row, swinging her small legs absently and looking around the sacred space with curiosity.

"Pastor Williams," Emma's father said respectfully, standing as they entered the quiet chapel. "You mentioned someone had information specifically about the angel who saved Emma?"

The pastor nodded affirmatively, stepping tactfully aside. "These people requested to speak with you privately about a matter of great importance. I'll leave you to talk in confidence, but I'll be just outside if you need anything at all."

As he left discreetly, closing the heavy wooden door behind him, Emma's eyes fixed intently on Calista, widening slightly.

"Thank you sincerely for coming on such short notice," Calista began, her voice steadier and more confident than she had expected. "My name is Calista Wright. This is my supportive friend Erica Butler, and my professor and mentor, Dr Mercer."

"I'm Thomas Phillips," Emma's father said cordially. "This is my wife, Diane, and our daughter, Emma."

"You're her, aren't you?" Emma said suddenly with childlike directness, sliding eagerly off the polished pew and taking a small, tentative step forward. "You're the angel lady who saved me."

The refreshing directness of a child, unfiltered by social conventions. Calista smiled warmly, kneeling gracefully to Emma's eye level. "What makes you think that, Emma?"

"Your eyes," Emma said simply, studying Calista's face. "I remember them. And your hair."

Calista looked up at Emma's watchful parents, who were observing the interaction with a complex mixture of confusion and gradual dawning realisation.

"She's right, isn't she?" Diane asked softly, her voice barely above a whisper. "You're the one who miraculously saved her."

Calista stood slowly, taking a deep breath to centre herself. "Yes. I want you to be the first to know – officially. You deserve that much consideration and respect after everything you've been through."

"But you look... completely normal," Thomas said, clearly bewildered by the disconnect. "Where are the...?" He gestured vaguely, uncertainly towards her back, seemingly embarrassed to articulate the impossible.

"I can control precisely when they appear," Calista explained patiently. "Most of the time, they exist in what I've come to call the adjacent space – present but not visible in this particular dimension of reality."

"Can we please see them?" Emma asked eagerly, practically bouncing with excitement. "Please? Pretty please?"

Calista glanced uncertainly at Dr Mercer, who nodded encouragingly with quiet confidence, and at Erica, who gave her an enthusiastic thumbs-up from where she stood.

"Alright," she said with resolve, stepping deliberately back to give herself adequate space. "Try not to be alarmed by what you're about to witness."

She closed her eyes in concentration, focusing intently. The chapel's high, vaulted ceiling afforded her ample room to extend her wings fully, their pristine white feathers catching and refracting the coloured light streaming through the stained glass windows.

There were audible gasps of astonishment from the Phillips family, followed by a profound silence so complete Calista could hear her own rapid heartbeat. She opened her eyes cautiously to find all three of them staring in undisguised wonder at the impossible sight before them.

"They're absolutely beautiful," Diane whispered reverently, a trembling hand pressed to her mouth in amazement. "Like nothing I've ever seen before."

Emma approached slowly, her small face alight with pure, childlike awe and wonder. "Can I touch them?" she asked tentatively, her voice hushed with respect.

"Gentle touches only!" her vigilant mother interjected protectively.

Calista nodded her permission. "It's perfectly ok. You can touch them if you'd like."

Emma reached out with exquisite care, her small fingers brushing delicately against the downy feathers with unmistakable reverence. "So soft," she murmured with delight, unconsciously echoing Erica's first awestruck reaction. "Just like in my dreams about you."

Thomas remained rooted where he stood, his expressive face cycling visibly through profound disbelief, overwhelming wonder, and finally, unmistakable gratitude. "You saved our precious daughter," he said, his voice thick with powerful emotion. "We can never adequately repay you for that miracle."

"I don't want or expect repayment," Calista assured him sincerely. "I just want... understanding. I've spent my entire life hiding what I truly am, deeply afraid of how people would react if they knew. When I saved Emma that day, I exposed myself publicly for the first time, and now everyone seems to be looking for me, speculating about my existence."

"That's precisely why you came to us first," Diane realised with sudden insight. "Before going fully public with your extraordinary truth."

Calista nodded in confirmation. "I'm still figuring out exactly how much to reveal, and to whom. But I knew without question that I needed to thank Emma personally first, before anything else."

"Thank me?" Emma looked up, genuinely puzzled by the statement. "But you saved me from something terrible."

"Yes, but you also saved me, in a profound way," Calista explained thoughtfully, kneeling again to the girl's eye level. "You helped me realise I simply can't hide forever behind a façade. That maybe, just maybe, the world is finally ready to know about people like me, to accept differences they don't fully understand."

"Are there more exactly like you?" Thomas asked, his curiosity evident.

"Yes," Calista confirmed. "But I've never met another being like myself. My biological father was an angel, but I never actually knew him. My mother was entirely human."

"So you're essentially half-angel, half-human?" Diane asked, trying to make sense of the revelation.

"Yes. Pretty much."

Emma reached enthusiastically into her pocket and pulled out a carefully folded piece of paper. "I drew this for you," she said proudly, handing it to Calista. It was the colourful picture she'd shown publicly at the thank-you event – a vibrant rendering of Calista with distinctive pink hair and majestic white wings.

"It's absolutely perfect," Calista said, genuinely touched by the gesture. "Thank you so much, Emma."

"What happens now?" Thomas asked practically. "Are you planning to go completely public with this?"

"Gradually," Calista said, standing gracefully. "I'm meeting with a journalism professor from my university next to carefully control how the story emerges. But I wanted you to know first – personally. Also, I have an important favour to ask."

"Anything at all," Diane said immediately without hesitation.

"When the story inevitably breaks in the media, would you possibly consider speaking publicly about your personal experience? Not revealing anything I've told you in strict confidence, but simply confirming that we've met, that I'm... real and not a fabrication."

Thomas nodded without the slightest hesitation. "Of course. Whatever helps you navigate this challenging situation."

"People will undoubtedly have countless questions," Diane added thoughtfully. "Some will be deeply sceptical, others irrationally afraid of the unknown. Having us publicly vouch for you might help considerably." She smiled warmly. "We can be your character witnesses, testifying to your fundamental goodness."

Calista felt a powerful surge of profound gratitude towards this remarkable family who, despite the overwhelming shock of what they were witnessing, responded with such immediate, unhesitating acceptance of her true nature.

"Thank you," she said simply but sincerely. "That means more than you could possibly know."

After patiently answering several more of their understandably curious questions – no, she couldn't possibly fly all the way to the moon; yes, she attended regular university classes like any other student; no, she didn't possess a luminous halo – Calista prepared to leave. She carefully retracted her wings, the gleaming feathers dissolving seamlessly back into the adjacent space.

Emma hugged Calista impulsively, wrapping her small arms around her waist. "Will I definitely see you again?" she asked hopefully.

"Yes," Calista promised firmly. "This isn't a final goodbye. It's just the beginning of something new and wonderful."

As they left the peaceful sanctuary of the church, Dr Mercer placed a reassuring hand on Calista's trembling shoulder. "You handled that beautifully," she said with genuine approval. "Are you mentally prepared for the next significant step?"

Calista nodded determinedly, checking her phone for emails. Jackson and Professor Callahan had readily agreed to meet them at Dr Mercer's campus office at 4pm. "As ready as I'll ever be, I suppose."

Chapter Ten

The sprawling university campus was pleasantly quiet on Sunday afternoon, most students either studying diligently in their dormitory rooms or enjoying the last precious hours of the weekend elsewhere. Dr Mercer's office felt like a comforting sanctuary – neutral, professional ground for the potentially life-changing conversation to come.

Jackson arrived promptly with Professor Callahan, both looking intensely curious. Their expressions transformed dramatically to undisguised shock when Calista calmly explained exactly who she truly was and, as irrefutable evidence, briefly manifested her magnificent wings in the confined space of the cluttered office.

"I knew it," Jackson whispered triumphantly, his keen journalistic instincts thoroughly vindicated. "I instinctively knew there was something extraordinary about you."

Professor Callahan was considerably more measured and professional, asking thoughtful, penetrating questions about precisely how Calista wanted to proceed with the public revelation. Together, they methodically outlined a comprehensive approach: an exclusive, in-depth interview, published first in the respected university paper but with carefully negotiated rights to syndicate strategically to larger media outlets. Calista would retain full final approval on all content. Her sensitive personal details – her residential address, her detailed class schedule – would be scrupulously kept private.

"This is unquestionably the story of a lifetime," Professor Callahan acknowledged with professional respect. "But it absolutely needs to be told responsibly, in a carefully considered way that protects you while simultaneously satisfying legitimate public curiosity."

By the time they departed, a detailed plan was firmly in place. The comprehensive interview would happen the very next day, with publication strategically scheduled for Wednesday morning.

"Are you completely sure about this accelerated timeline?" Erica asked with friendly concern as they walked leisurely back to their apartment. "It seems extraordinarily fast for such a momentous revelation."

"Better to decisively control the emerging narrative quickly than let wild speculation run unchecked," Calista replied with newfound confidence. "Besides, Jackson had already essentially figured it out through his investigation. Others inevitably would too, given enough time. This way, the authentic story comes directly from me first."

That evening, Calista sat contemplatively with Erica at their small kitchen table, meticulously preparing for the upcoming interview. They crafted nuanced answers to likely questions, practiced clear explanations of her unique abilities, and thoughtfully discussed important boundaries – what she was and wasn't comfortable sharing with the world.

"What about spectacular flying demonstrations?" Erica asked pragmatically. "They'll definitely want that dramatic visual for the accompanying photos."

"I'm reasonably comfortable with that, as long as it's conducted in a carefully controlled setting with appropriate privacy," Calista replied, making a detailed note. "No public stunts or circus-like performances, though."

As the hour grew increasingly late, Erica thoughtfully prepared steaming herbal tea and joined Calista companionably on the couch. "Nervous about tomorrow's interview?" she asked with friendly concern.

"Absolutely terrified," Calista admitted candidly. "But also... strangely relieved? It feels right somehow, like a burden lifting."

"For what it's genuinely worth, I think you're unquestionably doing the brave, honest thing," Erica said. "Though this dramatic revelation means I'll have to find completely new material for my comedy sets. 'My flatmate never properly does the dishes' will hit very differently when everyone knows she can literally fly."

Calista laughed appreciatively, deeply grateful for the much-needed moment of comforting levity. "I'm certain you'll manage to adapt your material successfully."

"Oh, I definitely will," Erica assured her confidently. "Living with an actual angel is absolute comedy gold waiting to be mined. The societal bar for celestial flatmates is unreasonably, impossibly high, you know."

They sat contentedly in comfortable, companionable silence for a while, sipping their tea, before Erica spoke again, her tone noticeably more serious and reflective.

"You fully realise this fundamentally changes absolutely everything, right? Your ordinary life won't be remotely the same after Wednesday's publication."

"I know," Calista said softly, thoughtfully. "But I don't think it realistically could have stayed unchanged anyway. Not after the highly public rescue." She looked out the window at the star-studded night sky. "My mother always told me to hide completely, to blend seamlessly into human society. She was genuinely trying to protect me from danger.

But I think... I think maybe she was wrong. Not about the very real risks – those certainly exist – but about the possibility of eventual acceptance."

"Your cautious mother didn't know me," Erica said with assurance. "Or the compassionate Dr Mercer. Or the remarkably understanding Phillips family. You've already assembled a pretty solid, reliable support team, Cal."

"I truly have, haven't I?" Calista smiled gratefully, feeling a powerful surge of profound gratitude. "Whatever unexpected challenges happen next, I won't be facing them alone."

Epilogue

The interview, when it finally happened on Monday afternoon, proved to be far less daunting than Calista had anticipated. Professor Callahan guided the conversation with skilful professionalism, ensuring Jackson's eager questions remained respectful and thoughtful. Calista answered each one with a newfound confidence, her voice growing steadier as the interview progressed. When the time came for photographs, she stood in the empty university quad, the setting sun casting a golden glow across her features as she unfurled her magnificent wings.

"Perfect," Jackson whispered in awe as the camera shutter clicked rapidly. "Absolutely perfect."

The article was published on Wednesday morning as planned, first in the university paper and then syndicated to major news outlets across the country by afternoon. Calista had braced herself for chaos, for overwhelming public scrutiny and judgment, but what followed surprised her in the most wonderful way.

The response was overwhelmingly positive. Where she had expected fear, she found fascination. Where she had anticipated rejection, she discovered reverence and respect. Students smiled at her as she walked across campus, some approaching with genuine curiosity rather than sensationalism. Professors nodded in acknowledgment, treating her no differently in class than before. The predicted media frenzy was tempered by the careful groundwork Professor Callahan had laid, ensuring most coverage remained dignified and factual.

"I told you so," Erica said smugly one night a month later, sprawled across their living room couch after returning from a successful stand-up set at a local comedy club. "People are better than you feared they'd be."

"You were right," Calista admitted. "Not everyone, of course. There are sceptics and a few fringe groups with... concerning interpretations. But most people have been remarkably accepting."

"Speaking of acceptance," Erica said with a grin, "my 'Living with an Angel' material rocked at the club tonight. The bit about finding feathers clogging the shower drain had them howling."

Calista laughed. "Who knew my celestial heritage would inspire your comedy?"

"I always said you were my guardian angel," Erica quipped, reaching for her laptop. "Oh, and Emma's mother stopped by earlier. They want to know if next Saturday works for Emma's birthday party."

The Phillips family had remained a constant presence in Calista's life. What began as a dramatic rescue had blossomed into a deep and meaningful connection. During a quiet dinner at their home, Emma had shyly asked if Calista would be her godmother.

"We can't think of anyone better suited," Thomas had explained, his eyes warm with genuine affection. "Someone to guide her spiritually seems particularly fitting, given... well, everything."

Calista had accepted through tears of joy, overwhelmed by the beautiful symmetry of it all.

Her academic life continued with surprising normalcy. Dr Mercer remained an invaluable mentor, guiding Calista's studies with the same thoughtful wisdom she had shown throughout the revelation process. Together, they had begun researching historical accounts of celestial encounters, separating mythology from potential truth, creating a scholarly framework for understanding literary depictions of the supernatural. "Your courage opens doors for others who might be hiding still," Dr Mercer had said one afternoon.

It wasn't always easy. There were difficult days when the attention became overwhelming, when well-meaning strangers asked invasive questions, when religious groups sought her endorsement for their particular interpretations. But Calista navigated these challenges with growing confidence, setting boundaries when needed, declining interviews that felt exploitative, refusing offers that would turn her into a spectacle.

She declined numerous offers to monetise her identity – reality shows, book deals promising sensational revelations, endorsement contracts for products ranging from energy drinks to luxury jewellery. Instead, she channelled her unique platform into meaningful advocacy, speaking occasionally at conferences about acceptance and diversity in its most profound sense.

On the anniversary of her public revelation, Calista stood on the roof of her apartment building at sunset, wings fully extended, feeling the gentle breeze ruffle her feathers. The city sprawled below her, golden light reflecting off windows and creating a breathtaking mosaic of human life. She thought of her mother, who had taught her to hide out of love and fear, and wondered what she would think of the path her daughter had chosen.

Calista spread her wings wider, catching the wind, feeling the familiar exhilaration as she prepared to take flight. She was no longer hiding, no longer constrained by fear and secrecy. She was no longer an angel in disguise, but simply Calista Wright: student, friend, godmother – occasionally spectacular but fundamentally ordinary in all the ways that truly mattered.

As she soared above the city, she caught sight of a small gathering in a park below. She dipped her wing in greeting, heart full of gratitude for the unexpected journey that had brought her here, to this perfect moment of belonging, acceptance, and joy.